Themba

Also by Margaret Sacks

Beyond Safe Boundaries

Themba

by Margaret Sacks
illustrated by Wil Clay

Lodestar Books

Dutton   New York

for David and Wendy

Text copyright © 1985, 1992 by Margaret Sacks
Illustration copyright © 1992 by Wil Clay

Library of Congress Cataloging-in-Publication Data

Sacks, Margaret.
   Themba / by Margaret Sacks; illustrated by Wil Clay.
—1st American ed.
       p. cm.
   Lodestar Books.
       Summary: Themba, a young South African boy, devises a plan to
bring his father home safely after he fails to arrive on the train as expected.
   ISBN 0-525-67414-4
   [1. Fathers and sons—Fiction. 2. Blacks—South Africa—Fiction.
3. South Africa—Fiction.]
I. Clay, Wil, ill. II. Title.
PZ7.S1223Th 1992
[Fic]—dc20   92-9754
                                                                  CIP
                                                                   AC

First published in the United States in 1992 by Lodestar Books,
                an affiliate of Dutton Children's Books,
                a division of Penguin Books USA Inc.,
          375 Hudson Street, New York, New York 10014

Published simultaneously in Canada by McClelland & Stewart, Toronto

Originally published in South Africa in different form as
                   Themba Fetches His Father
              by Human & Rousseau (Pty) Ltd.

Printed in the U.S.A.
ISBN 0-525-67414-4
First American Edition
10 9 8 7 6 5 4 3 2 1

Themba sat up in his straw bed and put out his hand to touch the dark. Not even a ray of light entered the windowless, mud-walled hut where he lived.

"Today Father comes home to Iqoto," he whispered. Unable to contain his excitement any longer, Themba gently stuck his elbow into his brother's ribs, trying to nudge him awake. "Come on, Luthando, wake up. Don't you know what's happening today?"

Luthando grunted sleepily from his side of the bed they shared and then sat up rapidly. "Of course I know. Utata is finally coming home." Luthando was just as excited as Themba.

Their father—their *utata*—had been away from the village for three years, working in the gold mines near Johannesburg, a giant city about five hundred miles north of Iqoto. Both boys remembered the day their father had called them to him. They each sat on one of his knees while he explained that he had to go far away for a long, long time. His voice was low with sadness. "If I stay here, we will always be poor," he said. "In the gold mines I can make enough money that you children won't ever have to be hungry or cold. You'll have warm clothes and sturdy shoes in winter, and maybe one day you'll go to school in the city so that you won't end up as poor farmhands like your uncles and me."

"You want us to be like my friend Koos," Themba had said. Koos was farmer Marais' son, the same age as Themba. He lived with his family in the large brick farmhouse, where he had his own bedroom and ate his meals at a long oak dining room table. Themba and Luthando's father had worked on the Maraises' land since he was a young man, and their mother still worked in the Maraises' kitchen. Sometimes she would bring home tasty leftovers, usually meat, which Themba's family couldn't afford.

"Koos says it must be fun to live in a hut instead of a big house," Themba had said, hoping his father would change his mind.

His father smiled. "If you live in a big house, it probably would be fun for a night or two. But have you told your friend Koos how it is in winter when the frost creeps along the ground and bites your toes till you dance with pain?"

"Who's going to take us hunting and fishing when you're gone?" Luthando had wailed.

Won't it be fun to hunt and fish again with Utata," Themba whispered, remembering Luthando's concern when their father had left.

"Let's hope he hasn't forgotten his skill at the bottom of the gold mines," Luthando said.

A rooster crowed shrilly outside, and their mother stirred in her corner of the hut.

"Boys, this is a very special day," she told them.

"We know, we know," they said together.

"What time will Utata arrive?" asked Themba, although he had already been told a dozen times.

5

"Perhaps he'll come soon after midday if we're very lucky." His mother smiled. "The train from Johannesburg arrives in Queenstown at about nine in the morning. Then he has to catch the bus and walk several miles. Of course, sometimes the buses run very late and stop at different farms and villages."

"If we were rich like farmer Marais, we'd have a car and could drive to the station to meet him," said Themba.

"If we were rich, Utata wouldn't have left in the first place," Luthando reminded him.

"Very smart, my little one, but now it's time to collect firewood for breakfast," said their mother.

The two boys ran outside and were joined by the other village children. They collected bundles of wood and arranged them for the breakfast fire. The air smelled sweet, and the rising sun cast a pink glow over the landscape. The delicious smell of maize porridge made them hungry.

The villagers gathered for breakfast. Young women suckled their babies. The children sat eating, surrounded by hens puk-pukking for crumbs, while the grown-ups talked. Some boys aimed warm milk from a cow's udder directly into their mouths. Themba could see that his mother's thoughts kept wandering, for she hardly listened when people spoke to her.

"Time is moving like a fat slug," complained Luthando.

"So let's do something useful," said Themba. "We could make a big sign to welcome Utata. Maybe Koos can help us."

"I guess," Luthando said. He always felt left out when Koos and Themba got together. But fortunately for him, Koos attended boarding school in Queenstown and only came home some weekends.

"Hey, Themba, d'you want to go fishing?" a voice called from the dirt road above Iqoto.

"Speak of the devil," Luthando thought. Koos hadn't wasted much time in seeking out Themba, although Mrs. Marais wasn't too happy about his spending so much time with the farmhands' children.

"Maybe later," Themba replied. "My pa is

7

coming home today, so we're going to make a sign to welcome him."

Koos ran down the hill. "I'll help," he said.

The boys found a large, flat piece of wood and collected the prettiest, smoothest stones. Then they tore the sap from the bark of a blue gum tree until their hands ached.

"This is not sticking too well," Themba complained.

"Come up to the house and we can use my bottle of glue," Koos said.

"He has his own glue?" Luthando asked in Xhosa, the language of his people, so that Koos didn't understand. He thought of the one bottle of glue that all the students had to share at the mission school.

"Not only does he have glue," Themba told his brother. "You should see his bedroom. He has a desk piled with clean white paper, lots of pens and pencils, a big bed, a closet for his clothes, a thick rug on the floor, a bathroom and—" Themba tried to think what else Koos had. Themba had only been in Koos' bedroom one time, because Mrs. Marais said she

9

didn't want the farmhands' children wandering upstairs.

"You know I hate it when I don't understand what you're saying," Koos broke in. Themba and Luthando grinned at each other. They waited on the verandah while Koos went inside for the glue. They didn't want to bump into Mrs. Marais.

The glue worked beautifully, and the boys stood back to admire their handiwork—a stone mosaic that said WELCOME HOME FATHER.

"Let's hang it at the entrance to the village," Themba said. "Then we can go fishing. Luthando, you too."

It was noon when Themba and Luthando returned to their hut. They were astonished to see how lovely their mother looked. Her arms and neck were adorned with beautiful beadwork. She had made the necklaces and bracelets herself from tiny beads, cleverly woven to form patterns of many colors.

By mid-afternoon Themba and Luthando were growing stiff with waiting, but still there was no sign of their father. When the sun set and the sky turned to dusk, Themba wanted to cry.

"What's happened?" he asked their mother.

"Perhaps the train was too full, and he'll have

to come next Saturday." She didn't sound very sure of herself, and when he saw her anxious eyes and unsmiling mouth, he didn't ask any more questions.

"Sipho's *utata* never returned and neither did Nomsa's," Luthando whispered. "Koos says that Utata never should have left. He was the best farmhand they ever had."

"Of course," his mother said with fire in her eyes. "But did farmer Marais pay him a decent wage? Never! That's why we live in a village of women, children, and old people. All the young men have to leave home."

That night Themba tossed and turned and thought hard. Then he came to a decision. He woke his brother and whispered to him:

"Luthando, I have a plan. Can you keep a secret?"

"Of course," Luthando said seriously.

"Next Saturday I'll go to Queenstown to meet the train from Johannesburg, and if Utata doesn't arrive, I'll travel to the mines to find him."

Themba was a little afraid of his own plan,

but he knew he had to do something. After all, his name meant "The one you can rely on."

"I'll come with you," said Luthando.

"No, you must stay here, because if I'm not back by nightfall, you'll have to explain where I've gone."

All week Themba tried to ignore the knot in his stomach. While the other children laughed and played on their walk to the mission school, Themba was silent and thoughtful. He had confided his plan only to Luthando and Koos. At recess Themba never ate his lunch, but carefully saved it in a paper sack in his satchel. He was preparing for his journey. In class he couldn't concentrate.

By Friday, Mr. Ndlela, the teacher, had reached the end of his patience. For the umpteenth time he asked, "Themba, what is bothering you? Do you have ants in your pants that you can't sit still?" But once again Themba did not answer. Finally, Mr. Ndlela wrote a letter to Themba's mother asking if she could find out what troubled him. Themba had nothing to say to his mother when she read the letter and began asking questions. She called her younger son.

"Luthando, your brother won't tell me his problem. Perhaps you can. Has it something to do with your father not arriving? But why doesn't he eat at school? He comes home as hungry as a lion."

"Well, I suppose he's saving his school lunch for . . ." Luthando stopped talking when he realized he was about to give away Themba's plan.

"For what?" his mother urged him.

"Well . . . um . . . you see," Luthando stuttered. "We are planning a feast for when father returns!"

His mother did not look satisfied, but she asked no more questions.

That night, Luthando stayed close to his older brother, dreading the thought that he would have to sleep alone the following night and perhaps for many nights to come.

"I wish Utata hadn't gone away at all," Luthando said.

"Don't worry," his brother replied. "I'll find him one way or another."

Saturday dawned. Themba was awake before cock's crow. For a moment he wondered if he would have the courage to carry out his plan.

After breakfast, the village women collected the cooking utensils. All of the women—even those who had babies on their backs—lifted bundles of laundry onto their heads. They walked down to the riverbank to do their washing. The children splashed in the water and made up games, using sticks and stones. Everyone was too busy to notice that Themba was not there.

He remained in the village, watching the men

get ready for work in Farmer Marais' fields. Themba followed them at a distance along a path of red dust, until he saw the farmer's truck being loaded with vegetables and fruit for the weekly market in Queenstown. Themba himself carried a live hen in a basket, which his grand-mother had woven from straw. She often used it to carry a laying hen to the country store where she would exchange the bird for some pretty beads.

When the farmer was about to leave, Themba ran from his hiding place in the shadows and climbed over the low ledge at the back of the truck. He lay down flat and hardly dared to breathe.

He heard a shout. Had he been discovered? He lay in the truck and waited. But no, there was another reason for the delay. The farmer's wife had promised to give her friend, who lived five miles down the road, a swarm of bees. The farmhand fetched the hive and gently lowered it into the back of the truck. Themba lay very still. The hive landed a few inches from his face. He remembered his father's advice not to move

whenever he was in danger of being stung. A bee landed on his nose. Themba squinted and had to clench his fists to stop himself from shooing it away.

The farm road was rutted and stony, and Themba's whole body was shaken. As the truck mounted a rocky hill, a pile of corn came pelting down on him. He was almost smothered, and he struggled to breathe.

After what seemed like hours, the truck stopped at a farmhouse, and the beehive was lifted off. But Themba, lying against the side of the truck, half buried by corn, was not discovered.

When the truck started again, Themba sat upright and looked around him. The farmlands were a patchwork of color, and cows and sheep grazed peacefully on the green grass. Themba's mind churned like the dust stirred up by the wheels of the truck. He could taste the dust and feel it sting his eyes. He lay back against the pile of corn. Then he wondered if he was dreaming, for suddenly the truck was gliding along smoothly. He peered out and saw that the road was smooth and firm. On either side of the road were houses with fields in between. They were on the outskirts of Queenstown.

They entered the town, and Themba was amazed at the number of vehicles zipping past. All the shapes, colors, and sizes! And all the different sounds they made! The large cars seemed to purr, while the small ones roared. His favorite was the double-decker bus with writing and pictures on the outside. He watched, astonished, as all vehicles stopped at the same time and all the people crossed the road together. He wrinkled his nose at the gas fumes and decided he preferred the fresh country air.

The farmer stopped at the market. Themba climbed out quickly with his hen basket and food package. He watched the farmers laying out their produce. It made his mouth water.

"Which way to the railway station?" he asked a woman. He could hardly keep his eyes from a pile of red, juicy apples, stacked in wooden crates.

"Six roads up on the right," she replied. "And here's a little something for you." She picked

out the reddest apple Themba had ever seen. He thanked her and started walking quickly, swinging his hen basket.

Suddenly Themba stopped in his tracks and peered in a shop window. Who were those people in beautiful clothes who did not move or speak? He stuck out his tongue and made a face to see if they would shake a finger at him as his mother always did when he was being naughty. Then, pressing his face against the glass, he realized that they were dolls—dolls as big as people.

The station building looked like a dark, noisy cavern. Themba approached a man in a navy blue uniform.

"When does the Johannesburg train arrive?" he asked.

The station master studied a watch attached to a gold chain across his belly. "It'll be at least another two hours," he said. "Running mighty late today."

Themba stared at the gold watch chain. "Have you been to the gold mines?" he asked, pointing to it.

"No, no! This you can buy at the bazaar," the man said with a smile.

Themba watched the engines shunting back and forth. He was amazed at the number of railway lines crisscrossing one another, and he wondered how the engine drivers knew which lines to follow.

He had two hours to spare and wanted to find Koos. But he also needed to keep a check on the time. He went back to the man in uniform and asked two questions. First, Themba wanted to know where the bazaar was, and second, he wanted to know how to get to Queenstown Boys' Academy.

The O.K. Bazaars was easy to find, around the corner. On the sidewalk outside the store crouched a beggar wearing dark glasses and holding out a hat. "Please, *baas,* a few cents for a blind man," he chanted. Every now and again a bypasser would throw some coins into the hat. Inside the store, Themba walked from counter to counter, his eyes wide with astonishment. Never had he seen so many goods in one place. But where were the watches? He finally located them at the jewelry counter. "How much is this one?" he asked the narrow-faced lady at the counter.

"Five rand," she said.

"I'll give you a good laying hen in exchange for the watch," said Themba.

"That's not possible," the woman said coldly and turned away to help another customer.

Themba went outside and hopped from one foot to the other, wondering what to do next. He saw a man throw a few coins into the beggar's hat.

"How long does it take you to make five rand?" he asked the beggar in Xhosa.

The beggar shrugged. "That would take about six days."

"Phew!" Themba let out a whistle.

"What's the problem?" the beggar asked.

Themba explained he needed a watch but had no money to buy it. The beggar jiggled the coins in his hat. "I don't have enough to lend you, but you could borrow the watch," the beggar said. "When no one is looking, take the watch off the counter. Later you can bring it back. In fact, if you bring it to me, I'll return it for you."

Themba retraced his steps. In the store, he stared at the watch a long time and then picked it up as the woman at the counter was clasping a necklace around a young girl's neck. The young girl spun around just as Themba was holding the watch.

"Look, a thief!" the young girl shrieked.

Themba dropped the watch and ran through the store and out the door with half a dozen people chasing after him. He ran and ran, and when he turned around to see if anyone was still chasing him, he swore he could see the beggar roaring with laughter.

Themba stopped to catch his breath and look around him. Across the street was a large building surrounded by lawn, and on the lawn stood groups of boys dressed in the gray and blue uniform that Koos Marais wore when he returned home for weekends. On the front of the building was a clock that said 9:30, although it felt like hours since he had left the station. Above the clock was written QUEENSTOWN BOYS' ACADEMY.

In his excitement, Themba ran across the street without looking for oncoming traffic. A car honked, and Themba's chicken squawked. The boys laughed at him. "Playing chicken!" one of them shouted, flapping his arms and making a cawing noise.

Themba went over to another boy standing alone. Where will I find Koos Marais?" he asked.

"He's probably in the dorm," the boy said. "I'll take you there."

The boys' dormitory consisted of row upon row of beds.

"What are you doing here?" Koos asked, surprised.

"Remember, I've come to meet my father at the station, but the train is two hours late."

"You still planning to go to Johannesburg if he doesn't arrive?"

Themba nodded, but he could feel his tummy tighten again in fear.

"I'll show you a map of South Africa in my classroom, and you can see for yourself how far you'll have to travel."

The two boys walked over to the main school building. Themba had never seen so many classrooms before, and in each one were rows of desks. Amazingly, the desks had lids that opened, revealing that each student had his own set of books. How different this was from the mission school, which consisted of one classroom crammed with tables and a few books that the students had to share.

"Here's the map," Koos said. "You see, Johannesburg is this big dot up north, and Queenstown is this little dot way down south."

"What about the village of Iqoto?" Themba asked.

Koos laughed. "Iqoto is so small it's not even on the map."

Just then a teacher walked in. "Koos Marais, what are you doing in the school on a Saturday? I thought your father was coming to pick you up. And who is this boy?"

"This is Themba from my dad's farm. I was showing him Johannesburg on the map."

"Ugh! A terrible city," the teacher said. "The streets are full of drunks, beggars, and gangs."

"I think I'd better go back to the station," Themba said to Koos in a croaky voice.

"Yes, it's almost eleven o'clock," Koos said, looking at his watch. "I'd come with you, but my pa is supposed to pick me up soon, and he'll be mad if I'm not waiting." He put out his hand to shake Themba's. "I hope your pa is on that train, my friend."

As Themba approached the station, he heard a shrill, distant whistle. From afar the train looked like a toy, snaking its way along the curved tracks. As it approached, the rhythm of wheels beating against the steel tracks blocked out all other sounds. The huge engine steamed to a halt, and carriage doors were flung open.

Themba ran the length of the platform, looking at all the faces of people getting off. He ran toward a tall man carrying a suitcase. But then he saw that the man had a beard and was thinner than his father. And he was wearing a jacket and tie. Tears of disappointment

came into Themba's eyes. His father was not there. Taking a deep breath, he realized that he must carry out the next part of his plan.

He walked to the ticket office.

"One ticket to Johannesburg, please," he said.

The clerk raised his eyebrows. "That's an expensive trip, and a very long one for such a young fellow," he said.

Themba held up the hen basket. "I have brought you a good laying hen in exchange for the ticket."

The clerk smiled kindly. "We only accept money."

"Then I will sell my hen and bring you money," said Themba. He ran out and crashed into the tall, bearded man in a jacket and tie.

"Why such haste, young man?"

Themba collected his wits. "This chicken is for sale," he said eagerly. "I need the money to buy a ticket to Johannesburg."

"And why would you be going there?" the stranger asked.

"To fetch my *utata* from the mines. He's been gone a long time."

"This *utata* of yours, what does he look like?"

"He's tall, strong, and clean-shaven, the finest fisherman and hunter of our village." Themba spoke in a rush, and his eyes darted around, looking for another buyer for his chicken, someone who would show more interest in the chicken than in him.

The man took off his jacket and tie and put them down. He covered his beard with one hand. "Is this how your *utata* looks?"

Themba frowned. Now that he was finally paying attention, he realized that the man's voice was familiar. He walked around the stranger and examined him from every angle. Then a big smile lit up his face.

"Utata, it's you!" He danced about, clapping his hands, and quickly began asking questions.

"Slowly, slowly." His father laughed. "Three years is a long time, and we have much to talk about."

"Why didn't you come last week?" Themba asked.

His father shook his head. "The train was so full there wasn't even standing room."

Hand in hand, Themba and his father left the station. The hen, forgotten in the excitement, was left squawking on a wooden bench.

At dusk, Themba and his father reached the village. At the entrance was the beautiful sign made by Themba, Luthando, and Koos: WELCOME HOME FATHER.

Men and women, clad in brightly patterned blankets, were resting after the day's work, some smoking long pipes. The children listened to an elder telling tales of long ago.

As Themba and his father came into view, the villagers rose, one by one, clapping their hands, swaying their bodies, and stamping their feet in a welcoming dance.

Two figures broke from the group. Luthando, running as fast as he could, was

ahead. His mother, her arms outstretched to embrace her husband and her son, was close behind.

The celebrations went on long into the night. Themba's cousins sacrificed a goat in thanks for the safe homecoming. As the villagers sat around the fire waiting for the meat to cook, Themba's father told them tales about the big city of Johannesburg.

"Will you go back there?" Luthando asked.

"Ah, it's so peaceful here," his father said, looking up at the stars. "I think for now I have enough money to lease some land and start my own small farm. Perhaps we can make it a village project. But I'm afraid one day when you children are ready for high school we will have to move to the city so that you can get a better education and have the opportunities I never had."

"No more serious talk tonight," Themba and Luthando's mother said, and once again the villagers broke into song and dance until they were too weary to rejoice any more.

On the Saturday after the homecoming, Themba's uncle returned from the Queenstown market, proudly carrying a laying hen he had bought.

The hen looked strangely familiar. It followed Themba everywhere, clucking all the time. It almost sounded as though the bird was scolding him.